Lauren Child

Slightly

Invisible

Featuring **Charlie** and Lola

with a special
appearance by
Soren
Lorensen

For the original Marv
and his sister Martha and
his brother Vincent.

And

for Conrad and his brother Enzo.

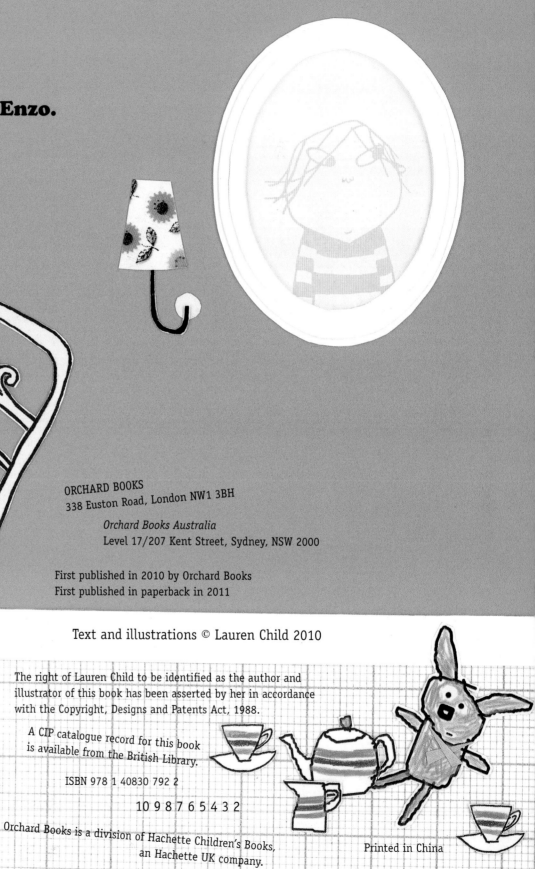

ORCHARD BOOKS
338 Euston Road, London NW1 3BH

Orchard Books Australia
Level 17/207 Kent Street, Sydney, NSW 2000

First published in 2010 by Orchard Books
First published in paperback in 2011

The right of Lauren Child to be identified as the author and
illustrator of this book has been asserted by her in accordance
with the Copyright, Designs and Patents Act, 1988.

A CIP catalogue record for this book
is available from the British Library.

ISBN 978 1 40830 792 2

10 9 8 7 6 5 4 3 2

Orchard Books is a division of Hachette Children's Books,
an Hachette UK company.

Printed in China

I have this little sister Lola.
She is small and very funny.
She always wants to know what I am up to and
she always wants to do what I am doing.
She NEVER wants to be anywhere without me.

Most of the time this is fine.
But sometimes I just want to be by myself
ON MY OWN with just Marv.

Marv is my best friend and usually we like
to spend our time looking for strange
and **tricky** creatures.

Lola does
not think
this is fun.

Last week Mary and me were busy floating in OUTER SPACE looking for the Martians,

and Lola stepped on our spaceship.

We had to **walk** back to Earth.

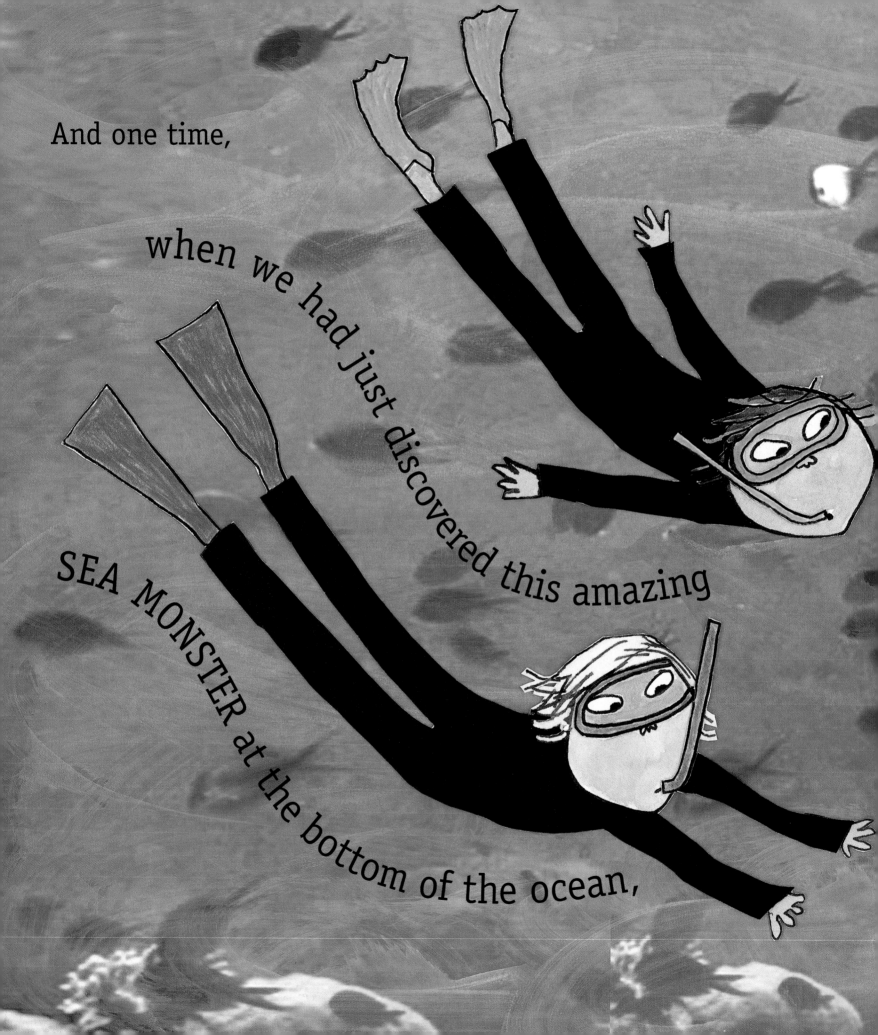

And one time,

when we had just discovered this amazing

SEA MONSTER at the bottom of the ocean,

Lola said she wanted to take it for a ride in her cart.

And yesterday,

just when

Marv and me

were

creeping up on the most STRANGE and

terrifyingly **tricky** creature in the UNIVERSE,

Lola's rabbit made a **squeaking** noise and he ran off.

So this time I said,

"Today Lola, just for once, I want to play with Marv by **myself** on my own.

You see we are inventing a very **inventive** invention."

"What **is** it?" says Lola.

"It's top secret," I say.

"What's it **top secret** for?" says Lola.

"It's a potion for helping us catch **strange** and **tricky** creatures," says Marv.

"Oh," says Lola. "How does it **do that**?"

"By turning you **invisible**," Marv says.

"Oh," says Lola. "Would you maybe like to have a **tea party** instead?"

"LOLA!" I say,
"Will you STOP bothering us
and interrupting!"

Lola says,

"I will NOT

do

bothering and I will NOT do interrupting. You won't even know I am here."

So
Marv and me
invent an **invisibility**
potion.

It is made from pink milk,

a tiny
drop of banana

and a **secret INVISIBLE INGREDIENT** that no one can see except us.

We leave it in the fridge and when we have sailed twice around the world and seen some EXTREMELY strange creatures

but not **one** single tricky one, we decide to have a snack.

Sailing around the world can make you quite peckish.

But when we go into the kitchen,
we get a bit of a fright

because there

is the

STRANGE and

terrifyingly tricky

creature

looking very hungry

indeed.

There is
no escape.

"Lola!" I shout, "What have you done with our potion?"
But Lola is nowhere to be seen.
We look **everywhere**.

But all we can hear is a tiny voice . . .

It sounds like it is coming from a long way away.

"where are you?"

I shout.

"I am over here, you **probably** cannot see me because I am **invisible**."

But
when I
look under
Mum and Dad's
bed there she is,
talking
away.

"Who are you talking to?" I say.

"My friend, Soren Lorensen,"
                                says Lola.

I say, "LOLA, did you drink our
                                invisibility potion?"
Lola says,
"Oh, I only had a small sip.
Soren Lorensen had much more than
                I did, that's why he is more
                                invisible than me."

I say, "You are NOT INVISIBLE,
not even one bit."

"How do you know?" says Lola.

"Because we can SEE you
of course," says Marv.

And Lola says,
"You can only see me because
you know what I look like.
You can't see Soren Lorensen
                                at all."

"That's because there is
NO such person as
Soren Lorensen," I say.

"Well, if there is
no such person..."

"Lola," I say, "now we will never catch the MOST STRANGE and terrifyingly **tricky** creature in the universe."

"Why not?"
says Lola.

"Because we can't CREEP UP on him," says Marv.

"Don't worry," says Lola, "Soren Lorensen will **catch** him."

"Really?"
I say.

"Oh yes," says Lola.
"All you will need is
a tea set
and a little cart
and also a rabbit of course."

"REALLY?" I say.

"Oh yes,
and you MUST
absolutely get one or
three glasses of
pink milk too."

"WHAT?
all of the
pink milk?"
says Marv.

"Yes,
completely,"
says Lola.

So we all set off to find the MOST STRANGE and terrifyingly tricky creature in the universe.

I say, "What is the tea set for, Lola?"

And she says, "Tricky creatures love tea."

And Marv says,

"What is the rabbit for, Lola?"

Soon we find ourselves right in the middle of the deep, dark forest where the MOST STRANGE and terrifyingly **tricky** creature lives.

And Lola whispers, "Sssh, Soren Lorensen is talking and **he says** we must be very, **extremely** quiet.

Don't make even a **squeak**."

"I can't hear him talking," says Marv.

"You can't **hear** him because he is INVISIBLE," says Lola.

"You CAN hear invisible people," I say.

Lola says, "Not Soren Lorensen because his **voice** is invisible **too.**"

Marv says, "There are no such things as **invisible** voices."

Lola says,
"If there are
no such things as
invisible voices,
then
why can't
you hear him?"

"SSSH," I whisper.
"Something is
coming."

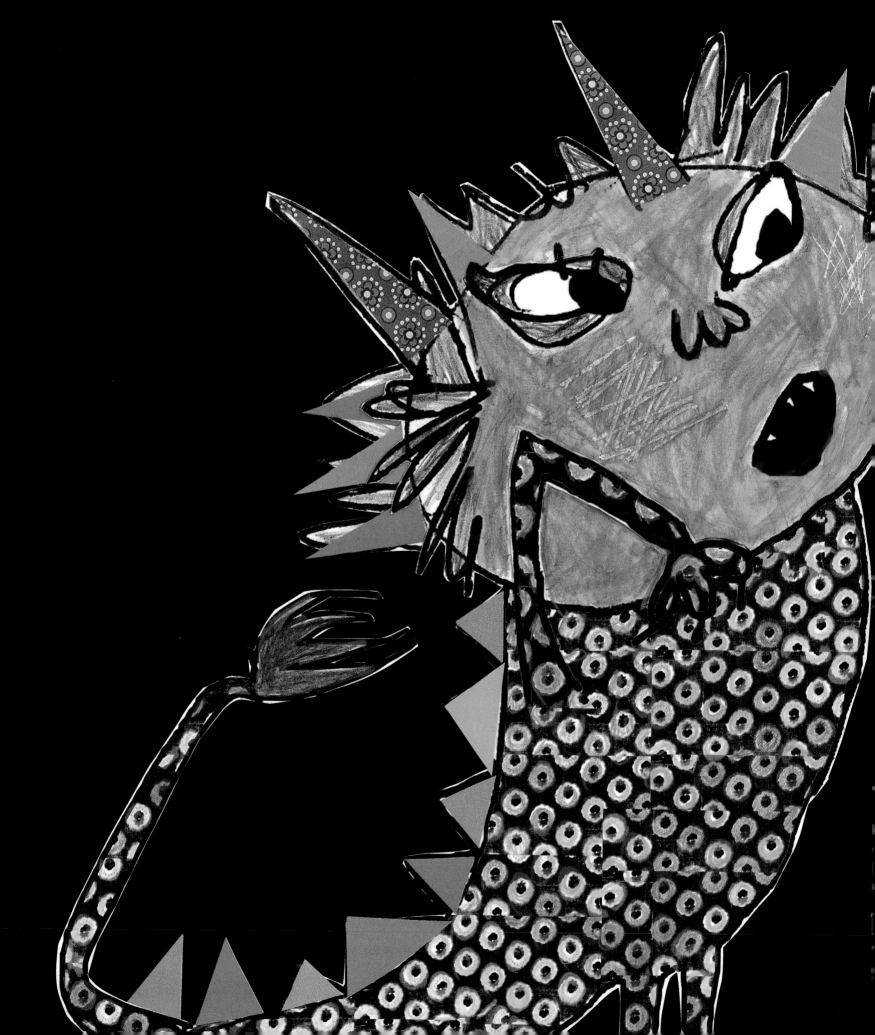

AND THEN THERE HE IS,

the most **strange** and terrifyingly **tricky** creature in the universe about to gobble us up . . .

"Show him the rabbit!"

says Lola.

And just like that

we have

CAUGHT

HIM.

And there is
no escape for
the MOST STRANGE
and
terrifyingly **tricky** creature
in the
universe.

"See!" shouts Lola,
"I **told** you Soren Lorensen knew how to
catch the most str∂ngest and
TRICKY creature."

"How did he do it?" I say.

"Well," says Lola,
"EVERYBODY loves **tea parties**."

"So who gets to drink the
pink milk?" says Marv.

"Oh, that is for
Soren Lorensen,"
says Lola.

"Catching strange
and **tricky** creatures
makes him quite
thirsty."

"Now," says Lola.

"It was fun to **play** with you and Marv, but please DON'T do **bothering** or **interrupting...**"

"Soren Lorensen would like to
drink his pink milk all by himself,
with just me on his own."